Spot's First Picnic

Eric Hill

A Spot Storybook

G.P. Putnam's Sons · New York

"They'll be here any minute, Mom!" Spot was going on his first picnic with Tom, Helen and Steve, and he was very excited.

He squeezed three peanut butter and jelly sandwiches into his backpack.

"I hope I haven't forgotten anything," said Spot as he licked his sticky paws.

Then he had an idea.

"Just what we need for our picnic!"
shouted Spot. And before Sally could stop
him, Spot had pulled the tablecloth off
the table – and everything with it.
Crash!

A knock at the door saved Spot from getting into more trouble.

"Your friends are here, Spot," Sally called. Spot rushed to the door.

"Hi, guys! Let's go. 'Bye, Mom!"

Sally looked up at the sky. It was cloudy. "Be careful," she told them. "And come back if it rains."

"Don't worry," said Helen. "I'll be in charge."

They climbed up a hill and Spot pointed
to a small wood on the other side.

"Let's go there," he said. "I know where
there's a stream and a big tree
we can sit under for our picnic."

"Come on. I'll race you to the stream!"

Spot got there first. Steve was second and Helen came in third.

Tom panted up last, but when he saw the water, he was the first one in. *Splash!*

Aaahh!

"It was silly of you to jump in like that, Tom," Helen scolded. "You might have hurt yourself."

"Well, I didn't," said Tom. "I'm cool now. Let's go eat."

Spot, Helen and Steve crossed the stream on stepping stones.

Spot put down the tablecloth and Helen unpacked the food. Tom rolled on the grass to dry while Steve climbed up the tree and watched.

They had just started to eat when it began to rain.

"Quick, everyone," Helen shouted. "Put the tablecloth over the branch and make a tent."

It was cosy and dry under the tablecloth, but Steve stayed outside.

"It's only a shower," he said as he climbed up on a branch.

Suddenly Spot heard Steve shout, "Ooops!" and the tent began to shake.

Then everything went dark.

Steve had slipped off the branch and pulled the tent down on top of everyone.

"That's the end of our picnic," moaned Spot. "It's all your fault, Steve," Helen complained. "You and your silly monkey tricks."

"We may as well go home," said Spot.

Sorry.

They packed up and started back across the stream. But the stones were slippery from the rain and Helen lost her balance.

"Help!" she cried. They all tried to catch Helen, but she fell and pulled everyone into the water with her.

What a mess! Spot looked around and started to laugh. "I guess this one was your fault, Helen. You and your silly balancing tricks!"

Everyone started giggling, and Helen laughed too.

"Wait until Mom sees us," Spot chuckled.

Sally had a surprise ready for them when they got home.

"I knew you'd come back wet and hungry so I made you an indoor picnic."